thuis – en heb bij het

et en aan – afschaduwi

e heb aangezet.

e nu geworden is

ek geschilderd

LOOKING *for* VINCENT

Thea Dubelaar & Ruud Bruijn

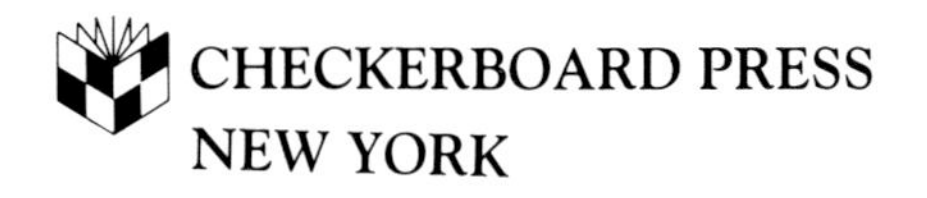

CHECKERBOARD PRESS
NEW YORK

I wasn't the least bit surprised when Aunt Elizabeth told me one day that she had fallen in love with a man who'd been dead for more than a hundred years. It was things like this that made me like going to see her so much—there was never a dull moment with Aunt Elizabeth around.

No sooner had I arrived than she showed me a painting of a thin man with a red beard. I thought he looked weird, but my aunt gazed at him in rapture.

"This is Vincent van Gogh," she said. "Doesn't he look marvelous?"

"Well, a bit old-fashioned perhaps," I mumbled.

"Don't go by the clothes. Look at the man inside them," she said. "And just look at what he painted." She showed me pictures of paintings of fruit trees in blossom, yellow fields of corn under blue skies, and trees so gnarled you'd think a whirlwind had blown through them.

"Anyone who could paint as splendidly as that must have been very special. Someone to love. I intend to find out all I can about him, and I want you to help."

"I don't have time today," I said quickly.

I don't understand
what she sees in him.

"Today is Wednesday," she reminded me. "You don't have school this afternoon."

"I've got soccer practice!" I replied. Aunt Elizabeth gave me a look that told me she knew I was making that up.

"No soccer today," she declared. "We're going to Amsterdam."

"To go around the canals on one of those tourist boats?" I asked hopefully.

"Maybe. If there's time. But first we'll start with the Van Gogh Museum."

A museum! I toyed with the idea of fainting on the spot and pretending to be really ill. Then I remembered the tourist boat and waited patiently for my aunt to put on her coat and get her purse.

"Did you bring money?" I asked. It would be just like my aunt to go out with no money.

It's a good thing I asked. She looked in her purse, but her wallet wasn't there. After a long search, we found it in the fridge.

The paintings of the weaver and the potato eaters from Vincent's dark period.

The Vincent van Gogh Museum was specially built to show the work of Vincent van Gogh and his contemporaries.

There wasn't much to see downstairs—some letters, photographs, and a few paintings—so we went upstairs. There we found Vincent van Gogh's early paintings. They were dark and somber and sad. Potatoes, baskets, and portraits of people so ugly you'd think they were caricatures.

They weren't at all like the brightly colored pictures Aunt Elizabeth had shown me. I stared in dismay at all the ugly faces. Aunt Elizabeth explained that these people, whom Vincent had painted, were poor peasants and weavers from the province of Brabant in the southern part of the Netherlands. They were so poor that all they ever had to eat were boiled potatoes with lard. They ate straight from the pot. Their homes were small and dark, lit only by a single oil lamp. Vincent painted reality as he saw it. I was glad to leave that gloomy gallery.

Next we came upon the painter's biography. I read that Vincent van Gogh was born in Zundert, an area in Brabant, in 1853. He was the eldest son of a Protestant minister and had two brothers and three sisters. He left school when he was sixteen. His uncle, an art dealer, got him work with the art dealer Goupil and Company. He worked for them first in The Hague, later in London, and finally in Paris.

Up close all you see are lots of brush strokes.
You need to stand farther away to see what the picture is.

Vincent didn't like selling art, and when he was twenty-three he left Goupil and Company to become a minister like his father and grandfather. At first he went to England where he taught school and became an assistant chaplain.

Later, in order to complete his studies, he was sent to preach in a coal-mining district in Belgium, where no one else would go. Vincent was extremely poor and virtually starved while he lived with the miners. But he stayed, preaching and drawing. Drawing had become as vital to him as breathing.

While he was there, his brother Theo came to visit and found him lying half dead on his straw mattress in a miner's hovel. Theo took him back to their parents' home. That was the end of Vincent's attempt at working for the church.

At that time Theo worked as an art dealer for Goupil's Paris branch. He believed that Vincent was going to be a great artist and encouraged him to draw and paint. Vincent and Theo agreed that every month Theo would send Vincent money to live on. In exchange, Vincent would send all his artwork to his brother to sell.

On July 27, 1890, Vincent van Gogh shot himself in a field. He died two days later. What gloom and misery had surrounded Vincent!

I looked at my aunt. She was still reading. I mumbled something about finding the bathroom and walked away. I got lost accidentally on purpose so I could wander around the museum. I took the elevator straight to the top floor where some Japanese prints were displayed. But I was more interested in the staircase. No sooner had I begun to slide down the banister than three security guards appeared. I quickly jumped down and went into another gallery.

I liked the brightly colored pictures I found there. The colors were overwhelming. I flopped onto a chair to recover from the colors. I thought about Vincent's last painting, of a cornfield with black crows circling in a blue sky. In a funny way, it seemed as if he hadn't painted the birds; it was as if the birds had flown onto the canvas and been transformed by magic into tiny black streaks of paint.

I wondered why Vincent had shot himself at a time when he was painting such happy pictures. What was Vincent thinking? I guess nobody will ever know.

Aunt Elizabeth broke into my thoughts. She had looked everywhere for me and at last had found me. She wanted to leave at once so she could get to a bookshop and buy all the books about Vincent she could find. It wasn't until I was in bed that night that I realized we hadn't been on the tourist boat.

This is one of Vincent's last paintings.

When I visited Aunt Elizabeth the next Saturday, her whole house smelled of oil paint. The living room floor was covered with a plastic sheet. There was a painter's easel with a canvas on it. My aunt stood behind it holding brushes and a palette. She'd been painting a bridge.

"It's the Skinny Bridge in Amsterdam," she told me. "I went to paint it yesterday, using Vincent's bridge as an example."

Then I saw on the floor all the books lying open to reproductions of bridges—not quite the Skinny Bridge, but a lot like it. One of them was the Pont de Langlois, in Arles, France, where Vincent had once lived.

"What do you think of it?" Aunt Elizabeth asked.

I was trying to think of some tactful way to say that her painting was a failure when she said, "Of course, it doesn't look like much, but then I only started painting yesterday. You can't compare my work with Vincent's." Then she showed me a still-life picture Vincent had done of a clog, a cabbage, and potatoes. The Brabant peasant period, I thought, proud of my new knowledge.

But I was wrong. Aunt Elizabeth told me that Vincent had painted the still life earlier on, when he was living in The Hague, a Dutch city on the North Sea, and taking lessons from his cousin Anton Mauve, a well-known painter. Mauve had handed him a canvas and paint, and told him to paint the still life in his studio.

I think the Skinny Bridge in Amsterdam
looks a lot like the bridge in Langlois, France.

"You wouldn't catch me starting with a cabbage and clogs for my first painting," I said. "I'd paint flowers."

"Or a bridge," said my aunt.

I nodded.

"Vincent had no choice," she went on. "He had to do what his teacher told him, and Mauve himself painted still lifes with a lot of brown in them. It was the fashion then. All paintings at that time were dark. Color, especially bright color, was considered vulgar and an indication of poor artistic technique. That may seem ridiculous now, but only a few painters dared to use color then—Gauguin, Degas, Monet. In fact, they used so much color it made them stand out. They were called Impressionists because of the way they painted their impressions of things in color.

"But Vincent didn't know about the Impressionists, and he obediently followed Mauve's instructions, even after they had had a fight.

"It wasn't until Vincent saw the paintings of Peter Paul Rubens, a seventeenth-century artist, in Antwerp, Belgium, that he began to long for color. It was at about that time Vincent discovered Japanese prints. They were totally unlike the respectable, dark Dutch paintings—bright yellow stood next to deep red, a stern blue-gray jostled a delicate pink. Green, orange, purple—all sorts of colors!

On the left is a print by the Japanese artist Hiroshige. On the right is Vincent's copy of it. Aunt Elizabeth told me that what Vincent had written down the sides in Japanese were the name and address of a business in Tokyo.

"Vincent dreamed of color, lots of color in his own paintings. He worked hard to master his art. There was no room, no time, no money for anything else in his life. Not even for a wife and children. Vincent was forced to choose between art and having a family of his own. He chose art. And now I know what my vocation is too," Aunt Elizabeth finished softly.

"Do you want to be an artist?" I asked.

She nodded. "Vincent's work has given me a passion for art. From now on, I want to live only for color, just as he did."

I stared at her in amazement.

"My life has been empty all this time," she said dramatically.

She made it sound as if she'd always been unhappy and lonely.

"Of course I'm not as talented as Vincent," she said, "but I intend to live until I'm a hundred, so I've got more time than he had to learn to paint." Then she looked at me and said, "If you started painting now, you could be even better. Here, let me give you some paints and canvas."

"I can't even draw," I exclaimed.

But my aunt wasn't listening.

The following Wednesday when I walked into my aunt's living room, she was waving a handful of money around in the air. I'd never noticed before that Dutch bills look like Van Gogh paintings from his brightest period. They're so colorful and beautiful!

"I'm going to buy one of Vincent's paintings," she told me happily. "There's one for sale and it's going to be mine!"

"At Christie's auction house?" I asked. Almost every time something by a famous artist goes on sale, it's at a Christie's auction. In 1987, one of Vincent's sunflower paintings sold for 39.9 million dollars at Christie's in London. As far as I knew, my aunt wasn't nearly rich enough to spend that kind of money. I could just imagine it: a whole row of millionaires with pocket calculators. Aunt Elizabeth sitting among them shaking the contents of her purse out onto her lap to count. The thought was so crazy I couldn't help laughing.

"I think you'd better empty your piggy bank," I jeered.

"I've done that," she answered, "and I've sold my pearls and your grandfather's gold watch."

"Oh, no," I groaned, "not Grandpa's watch. You promised me I could have it."

"First things first," said Aunt Elizabeth. "Vincent is more important than any watch. Besides, I can buy it back later."

"Wanting to own something of Vincent's is ridiculous!" I said angrily. "His work belongs in museums for everyone to see."

"There are more than enough paintings in them already," my aunt replied calmly. "No one will miss the one I want."

"It's absurd that his work's so expensive!" I ranted on. "Anyone who would pay that much for old art is out of their mind!"

"I think I'll buy one of those small leather pouches to hang around my neck," my aunt muttered, ignoring me. She stuffed the bundle of money into the pocket of her dress. It made an odd lump. I didn't feel like laughing now. I was furious about the watch.

"All you can think of is possessions, possessions, possessions," I snapped. I stalked over to the window and stood with my back to her.

"Perhaps you're right," she said after a while. She looked disappointed and guilty. "I can't compete with all those millionaires. And I can go to the museum every day to enjoy my beloved Vincent's paintings. Put on your coat. We'll go and buy back your grandfather's watch."

This is the painting that sold at an auction for $39.9 million. It now hangs behind bulletproof glass in a Japanese insurance company.

La Guinguette café terrace in autumn colors.

She looked excited as we walked down the street, but I heard her muttering, "What a pity, how I would have loved..."

I pretended not to hear. "Where are we going, anyway?" I asked after a while.

"To see Monsieur Christian," she replied. "He lives in a very special house."

Monsieur Christian's house looked ordinary enough from the outside, just another house in a row in an old neighborhood. But once through the front door, I stepped back in time. The rooms were filled with glossy polished furniture, the walls had flowery satin stuff on them, and curtains hung on the windows and the doors. Elegant vases filled with beautiful flowers were all over the place. Copies of works by famous Impressionists lined the walls.

"This is Paris a hundred years ago," my aunt whispered.

"Shall we sit out on the terrace, *ma chère?*" Monsieur Christian invited.

How fancy it all was. Aunt Elizabeth's face lit up when he called her "my dear" in French. With a proud and graceful air, Monsieur Christian led us to a room at the back of the house.

There an even greater surprise awaited me. The room was furnished with wooden tables and chairs in the style of an outdoor café, just like in old paintings. Painted on one wall was a beautiful mural with rooftops in the foreground and beyond it a city stretching into the distance.

"Paris!" Monsieur Christian said grandly. "We are standing on the Butte Montmartre, a hill in Paris. It used to be a village with vineyards and small houses and windmills. Ah, those splendid windmills that Van Gogh loved to paint."

"Vincent?" Aunt Elizabeth exclaimed. "Did he live here too?"

"In the rue Lepic," Monsieur Christian said solemnly. "That's where he had the studio and home he shared with his brother Theo. Quite a few artists lived in Montmartre at the time. They used to meet at Père Tanguy's where they bought paint and canvas. They liked going there because from time to time old Tanguy would put the young painters' latest paintings in his shop window. And if an artist was really without a cent, he exchanged paint and canvas for a painting. That man was indeed admirable."

Lost in thought, Monsieur Christian leaned on his silver-topped cane and looked out over Paris. "Ah, yes, those were fine times," he sighed. "I can't get used to how much Montmartre has changed. Houses everywhere, crowded streets, cars. Terrible! Compared with the atmosphere it used to have—terrible! Come, *mes amis*, let me invite you to Agostina Segatori's restaurant, the Tambourine."

Père Tanguy in front of a wall covered with Japanese prints. Vincent never painted Mrs. Tanguy. She didn't want her husband to give Vincent paint and canvas. Vincent called her names and said she was mean. Fortunately Tanguy helped him anyway.

Here we are with (from left to right) Eugene Delacroix, Emile Bernard, Vincent and Theo (standing at bar); and Claude Monet, Agostina Segatori, Monsieur Christian, Paul Gauguin, John Russell, Camille Pissarro (seated). And the dog!

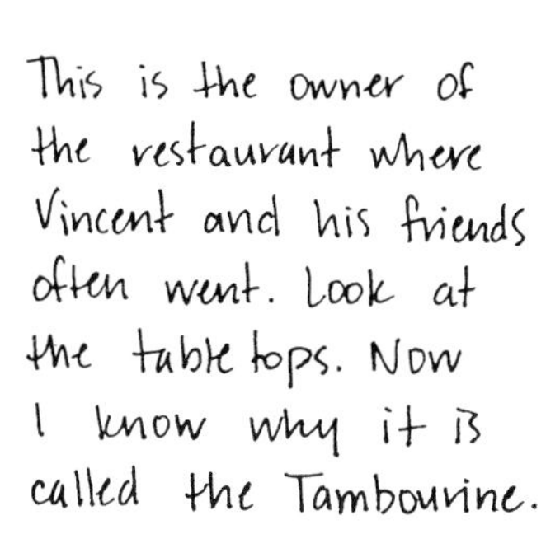

This is the owner of the restaurant where Vincent and his friends often went. Look at the table tops. Now I know why it is called the Tambourine.

He opened two frosted-glass doors. Suddenly it was as if we had stepped into a painting of an old-fashioned café. I recognized Vincent and Theo, who were leaning on the bar. Other men were standing around and sitting at tables. There was a woman, too. They looked as if they were talking to each other and having a good time. They were wax models—but they seemed so alive!

Aunt Elizabeth muttered their names to me: "Russell, Gauguin, Pissarro, Delacroix, Monet, Bernard...And who's that?" she said aloud. "Why it's you, Monsieur Christian."

"Ah yes..." Monsieur Christian faltered, blushing. "A little vanity of mine. Sometimes I really feel that I belong to that period.

"In the days when I worked as a scene painter at the historical museum in Montmartre, I used to sit perfectly still among the wax models in the middle of the scenery, staring blankly ahead as if I were a wax model, too.

"Just think of it! Unfortunately, when I turned sixty-five they sent me home to enjoy my old age. They said I could have some discarded stuff from the museum. I made these wax models myself. The rest of the furnishings I bought. I've spent every cent I had on them. Now I'm happy to quietly live in the Montmartre of a hundred years ago....

"Please, sit down. I'll get some wine."

We sat at one of the tables close to the glass doors with a view of the whole restaurant. Monsieur Christian left us and soon returned with a bottle of wine and grape juice for me.

I filled my glass and looked around. I thought about the dark room of the poor Brabant potato eaters compared with this lively restaurant full of special people. It was no wonder Vincent's style of painting changed.

"Tell us some more about Vincent," Aunt Elizabeth said, giving Monsieur Christian a smile.

Monsieur Christian took a sip of wine, cleared his throat, and settled down into his chair.

"Well," he began, "for some time Vincent had intended to live with Theo in Paris. He thought it would be cheaper

Vincent painted a self-portrait on the back of this still life of bottles and a bowl. Maybe he didn't like the bottles? Or maybe he didn't have enough money for new canvas?

Look at how Vincent's style has changed.

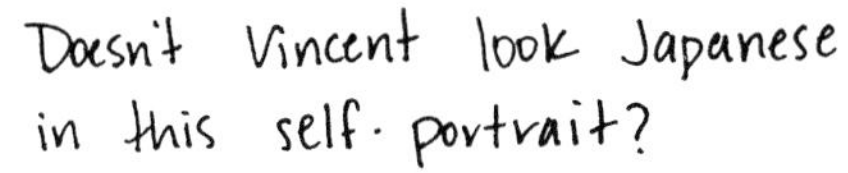
Doesn't Vincent look Japanese
in this self-portrait?

because they could share the rent. Buying food for two would be cheaper, too. Theo wasn't sure it would work. But Vincent was in a hurry to leave Antwerp, Belgium, where the painting class he'd been taking had ended. He had no money to pay models and didn't like painting outside in the cold of winter. Maybe that's why he painted himself so often. Of the 867 paintings he did in nine years, 37 are self-portraits.

"When he arrived in Paris at the beginning of March 1886, he sent a note to Theo at work. It said:

Forgive my sudden arrival; I've thought about it long and hard, and I believe we'll gain time this way. I'll be at the Louvre at twelve o'clock or earlier, as you wish. Please let me know what time you can come. I'll be in the Salle Carrée. Come as quickly as you can.

With a handshake,
Vincent

It's hard to believe that Vincent painted this.

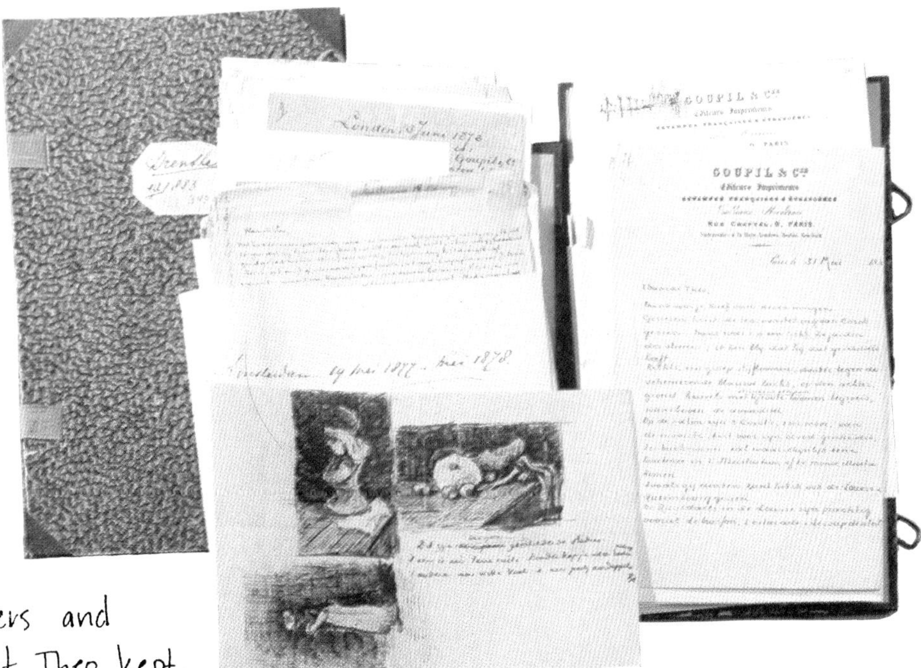

Some of Vincent's letters and drawings that Theo kept.

"Like all the letters Vincent ever wrote to his brother, the note has been saved. These letters tell us an amazing amount about Vincent.

"Before long Vincent went to the painter Cormon's studio, where he could work on life-drawings using nude models. There he met other artists—many became good friends.

"At the same time he began painting flowers. Listen to what he wrote to Livens, the English painter, that fall.

I've painted a series of color studies. Just flowers—red poppies, blue cornflowers and forget-me-nots, white and red roses, yellow chrysanthemums—all the time looking for the contrasts between blue and orange, red and green, yellow and purple, shades and neutral colors, seeking to reconcile the extreme contrasts. I've also done a dozen landscapes in a distinctive green and a distinctive blue."

Monsieur Christian put down the book. "In this letter Vincent sums up what happened to his painting in Paris. He turned away from the dark colors he'd been using earlier and began to use colors that were increasingly bolder and more powerful.

"His talent became more and more obvious, though not to the respectable patrons of Goupil and Company, who thought his work was loud and sloppy. But other artists who went to the studio were delighted to exchange their paintings with Van Gogh. Paul Gauguin in particular was a great admirer of his. And Vincent in turn was crazy about Gauguin's work. Unfortunately, Gauguin left Paris and went to live in the French countryside.

"By then Vincent had also had enough of Paris. He'd been there two years and had begun to feel like a carriage horse trotting pathetically over the dusty cobbles of the noisy city. He longed for the fresh green countryside with its peace and clean air.

"Van Gogh wanted to go south. He dreamed of the sun, of olive trees, of hills covered with vineyards.

"In the spring of 1888, Vincent left Paris and went to Arles, a town in the south of France. Theo was relieved. Vincent was a poor roommate. He was messy and selfish and had a bad temper.

"Vincent was happy to leave Paris. The south of France was like Japan to him. He wrote to Theo:

It's all so very colorful here. If you want to imagine how my paintings have changed, think about those Japanese prints.

"In Paris, Vincent had bought lots of Japanese prints and decided that Japanese art was pure, simple of line, and incomparable in color. He wanted to paint in the same pure, colorful way. In fact, Van Gogh produced three Japanese prints.

"Yes, Vincent was one of a kind. No one behaved like him. He was a misfit. A misfit and a genius."

A pear tree in blossom.

A cornfield with blue irises, which was just like a Japanese dream for Vincent. In one of his letters he said that he hoped they wouldn't mow the field too soon. He wanted another chance to paint it.

"I'm crazy about him," Aunt Elizabeth said, "really crazy. You've given us a wonderful afternoon with your stories, Monsieur Christian, but we must go now."

"Don't forget the watch!" I whispered.

"Oh, yes, the watch," Aunt Elizabeth said. "That's why we came. Dear Monsieur Christian, I would like to buy back the watch. Mark reminded me that I'd promised it to him, and a promise is a promise." And she gave Monsieur Christian her sweetest smile.

"True enough," said Monsieur Christian, "though I can't say I feel particularly like selling it. It suits me so well."

I looked him over from top to bottom but could see no sign of my grandfather's watch.

"I'm talking about the wax me," he explained. And there it was—the wax Monsieur Christian was wearing Grandpa's watch.

"You promised Aunt Elizabeth she could buy it back!" I said angrily.

"Calm down, Mark," said my aunt.

Monsieur Christian muttered, "I hadn't expected it to be so soon...Ah, well, if I must, I must." He stood up, removed the watch from the model, and handed it to Aunt Elizabeth. He was very disappointed, that much was clear. But he was still friendly and

even called out "*Au revoir*" when we left. Aunt Elizabeth told me that meant "See you."

As soon as we got home, my aunt announced, "I want to go to Arles. Not really, of course, but through my books and prints." So we pored over the pages of paintings Vincent had done in the south of France. He had begun very calmly with delicate colors and fine pencil lines. Sometimes he used dots to represent trees in blossom. After the dirty streets and houses of Paris, the trees of Arles at springtime

were so beautiful that Vincent just had to paint them.

In Arles, he became close friends with Roulin the postman. Roulin found a yellow house for Vincent to rent so he was able to leave the inn where he had been paying more than he could afford for a small room. Vincent made the ground floor his studio and furnished two rooms upstairs as bedrooms, one for him, the other for his friend Gauguin, whom he had invited to live with him.

That summer Vincent painted outside in the burning sun almost every day. He painted fertile fields and dazzling landscapes with houses and hills in the background. He went to Saintes-Maries, a village by the sea, and painted splendid pictures of boats with sea and sky.

Gradually his colors brightened. Finally, in midsummer, the sunflowers came out. Vincent painted one, then three, then a vaseful, and finally a bouquet. He was crazy about yellow. The bright yellow paintings were for Gauguin's room, a surprise for him.

Vincent painted the boats in Saintes-Maries, a seaside village. He used to wear his famous straw hat there. It is said that he even wore it at night with burning candles on the crown for light. I don't think I believe that.

Vincent was now painting day and night. He spent all his money on paint and canvas. Often there wasn't enough left over for food. Sometimes he would live for three or four days on just coffee and bread. He made paintings of his house, the town square, the vineyards, the café with tramps asleep outside under the stars. He painted with more and more yellow, until his whole life was dominated by it.

At last Gauguin arrived. It was the end of October 1888. Now that his friend Gauguin was with him, he thought they would paint the finest things together. Gauguin stayed exactly two months and then decided to return to Paris.

Vincent had a wild character. But Gauguin, too, was pretty extraordinary. They may have been the best of friends, but the yellow house wasn't large enough for two people like them. They fought endlessly, but when Gauguin decided to leave, Vincent couldn't bear it. Distraught, and already weakened by an irregular, skimpy diet, he completely lost control. He cut off part of his ear and went to bed to bleed to death. Fortunately, Roulin found him. Later, when he was recovering in the hospital, Van Gogh didn't even know how or why he had done it. He was confused and very unhappy.

Street café in the evening at the Place du Forum.

The people of Arles were afraid of the mad painter and demanded that he be locked up in an asylum. The police took him away. Vincent ended up in the asylum at Saint-Rémy, northeast of Arles.

My aunt and I leafed through the pages looking at the pictures. We soaked up the colors that exploded from the pages. My head was spinning with colors as I walked home.

"Sunflowers, sunflowers!" my aunt cried the next time I visited her. "Fields full of yellow flowers so bright they make you giddy, and above them the sun, blazing hot and golden. All I can think of is that golden yellow, the emperor's color, forbidden to ordinary mortals, the color of madness. I want to wallow in yellow. I want sunflowers, all over the house."

The walls of the living room were already covered in large yellow flowers. My aunt had been working like a demon.

Personally, I found all that yellow a bit much. It was as if the sun was shining from all the walls at the same time, as if the sky itself had become yellow. All that yellow made me want to throw up so I fled.

I wonder if Vincent forgot all about bright yellow when he did this melancholy painting of himself without his ear.

But from that moment on, Vincent never left my thoughts. I spent hours looking at books of his pictures I borrowed from the library. I found some colored transparent paper and began playing with it. I had only three colors—red, yellow, and blue. When I put them next to or on top of one another, something happened that was like Vincent's paintings, especially with the yellow. I needed a lot of yellow and a fair amount of blue, which turned green when I put it over the yellow. In this way I made yellow-green portraits in Vincent's style of my family from photographs.

After school the following day, I went straight to my aunt's house. I found her standing in front of her bedroom mirror wearing a sweatsuit and a pink wool hat. She had a scarf tied over her mouth. At first I didn't recognize her. When she saw me, she pulled off the scarf and tore the hat from her head.

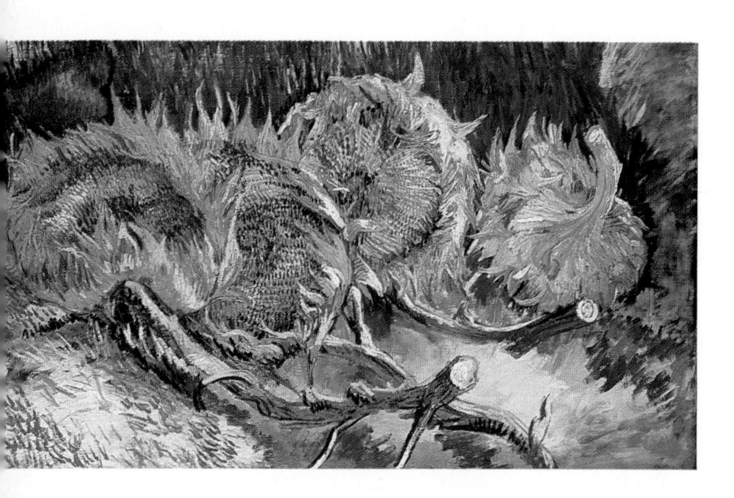

This painting of dried sunflowers was stolen from a museum. It's back now!

"What are you doing?" I asked in amazement.

"N-nothing," she stammered.

"You looked as if you were about to commit a bank robbery."

"Me?" She looked at me so innocently that I immediately felt suspicious.

"Are you going to break in somewhere?" I asked.

"Now where would I want to break into?" she replied.

"A museum? The Van Gogh, perhaps, or the Kröller-Müller?"

My aunt rushed over to me. She gripped my hands and stared deep into my eyes. "Mark, I can't live any longer without having something of Vincent's. I have to have something to touch so that I can feel his genius. After all, other people have managed to take something. Three paintings vanished from the Kröller-Müller Museum not so long ago."

"What's come over you," I hissed.

My aunt blushed furiously. "But I love him!" she whispered hoarsely. She looked desperate. I kind of understood. I couldn't get Vincent out of my mind, either. Even so, she had to get this crazy idea out of her head.

"You'll never pull it off," I said, imagining Aunt Elizabeth picking her way through the bushes to the Kröller-Müller Museum. The idea was ridiculous. "They've put in new alarms since the last break-in. Even professional thieves couldn't pull it off now. You don't have a chance. They'd catch you at once."

"Oh, heavens, what am I going to do?" Aunt Elizabeth wailed.

"I'll think of something," I promised. "Only please don't do anything without warning me first."

She nodded.

I ♥ ART

I left her sitting on the edge of the bed and headed for home. I felt uneasy. My nutty aunt was prepared to become a burglar. The thought of her ending up in prison! I needed to think.

Perhaps...An idea floated into my head. Perhaps Aunt Elizabeth could buy a fake with her savings and the money from the sale of her pearls. No, not a fake, a copy, made by a real artist, someone who could really paint a Van Gogh.

I can't believe that once he'd done twelve drawings for his uncle, an art dealer. But instead of paying Vincent the thirty guilders he'd promised, his uncle paid only twenty because, he said, the drawings had no commercial value. Now, a hundred years later, my aunt couldn't even buy one of his smallest drawings!

You can just see a bit of the asylum. The garden's beautiful. Just the same, I wouldn't want to be there.

It seemed unfair. All his life Vincent had been poor. He never had enough money to buy paints or canvas. Sometimes he couldn't even work because he'd run out of supplies. His health suffered because he didn't eat enough. All this time he felt he had to produce lots of good paintings so that one day Theo could sell them and earn back all the money he'd given Vincent. The idea of such a large debt worried Vincent all the time.

As I strolled along, I passed an old railway bridge. A rusty old car had been dumped nearby. The whole place seemed deserted. A lonely cat meowed hungrily at me. How would Vincent have painted *this*, I wondered.

I thought about the time Vincent had spent in Saint-Rémy. Although the asylum had seemed like a prison, he had worked very hard—in fact, in a little more than one year he had produced 190 paintings and 108 drawings!

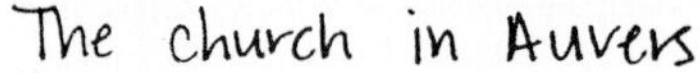

The church in Auvers

Madame Ginoux

He painted twisted olive trees, swaying cypresses–churchyard trees–outlined in black. He also painted ivy in sunny woods, fields of flowers, and a portrait of Madame Ginoux, the only person in Arles who always remained a friend.

Each time he thought he was getting better, he had a relapse. He became confused and struggled to paint with a clear head, a sure hand, and visions full of color.

Finally, he could bear Saint-Rémy no longer. On May 4, 1890, three months before he died, he wrote to Theo:

This place is beginning to suffocate me more than I can say. I need air. I'm being consumed with boredom and sorrow here. My patience is at an end, dear brother. I've had enough. I need a change, even if it's for the worse.

What can you do if your brother writes you a letter like that?

Theo brought Vincent back to Paris and then took him to Auvers, a village near Paris, where there was a good doctor, Paul-Ferdinand Gachet, who had many artist friends. He agreed to look after Vincent.

Theo returned to Paris, to his wife and their newborn son, named Vincent.

Vincent! To think I hadn't even heard of him until recently.

When I next visited my aunt, I remembered my good idea. "Why don't you buy a copy of one of Vincent's paintings?"

She perked up at once. "You're marvelous, Mark!" she cried. "I know exactly where to go for one. Demoker's."

The following Saturday off we went again by train, not to Amsterdam this time, but eastward. As the train raced along, Aunt Elizabeth told me about Demoker.

When his mind cleared, Vincent painted thirteen canvases in two weeks. This cypress is one of the paintings.

He'd had no success as a painter, so he decided to copy famous paintings and pass them off as originals. Technically, he was very good, and the Picassos, Monets, and Van Goghs he produced were so authentic that even experts were fooled. Inevitably, he was caught and sent to prison for fraud. He became quite famous.

When he was released from prison, he found work immediately. This time there was a difference; he signed the copies with his own name. There's nothing illegal about making signed copies. He was very successful.

"Won't he be expensive?" I asked.

"Don't worry. I've brought a fair amount of money with me," Aunt Elizabeth replied. I thought about the wad of bills I'd seen her hide in her pocket. It had indeed been a lot.

We took a taxi from the station and drove through woods along a main road for a while. Then we turned onto a small dirt road and stopped at a large gate."This is it," said the driver. We got out. Tall trees grew above the closed gate and golden leaves floated down. Aunt Elizabeth rang the bell.

"Who's there?" A disembodied voice came from a speaker near the bell.

"I've come for a copy," my aunt replied.

"I'm sorry," the voice said. "You must make an appointment."

Click, the voice was gone.

I looked at my aunt and she looked at me. Then we nodded at each other and climbed over the gate.

"I hope they don't have a dog," Aunt Elizabeth muttered.

Demoker's house looked very similar to the parsonage in Nuenen, where Vincent's parents lived. He must have had it built that way.

Vincent's painting of the convent, especially the cloisters, is impressive. Look at how the corridor seems to go on forever!

Once the house came into view, we left the driveway and crept through the bushes. A glass room had been built onto the house.

"That's the studio," my aunt said. "That's where he'll be."

We were lucky. Bushes grew alongside the studio, so we could see inside without being seen by the people inside.

"Can you see the paintings?" my aunt asked in a whisper.

"It's like the Van Gogh Museum," I whispered back.

"I wonder why there aren't any Picassos on the wall," my aunt said. "That's what Demoker specializes in."

"Everyone seems to be arguing," I said, speaking normally since they wouldn't be able to hear us.

"They do look a little angry, don't they," said my aunt. A man in jeans and a sweater walked toward us from across the room.

"That must be Demoker," my aunt whispered.

I thought he'd seen us but all he did was open a window. That was perfect—now we could hear what they were saying. It was an international gathering. French and English were being spoken; and every now and then, Demoker swore in Dutch.

"What is that woman saying?" I asked.

"The woman is speaking French," my aunt answered, "and she's saying, 'Vincent is ours. He did his most important work in France. He died in France. Arles and Saint-Rémy are in France. The Van Gogh monument should be the concern of the French.'"

"We also want a monument to Van Gogh. After all, Japanese art influenced him," said a Japanese man in English.

"Vincent is French," insisted the Frenchwoman.

"Don't be ridiculous!" shouted Demoker. "Vincent is a purebred Dutchman right down to his fingertips. Every detail of his brilliant paintings is Dutch. He's not at all like those Frenchmen. Neither Monet, Degas, nor Toulouse-Lautrec worked as Vincent did."

The house where Vincent died is now a restaurant, or at least it was on the postcard Aunt Elizabeth showed me.

This long, dark painting shows that the Nuenen parsonage had a very big garden.

At that moment the sun broke through the clouds and shone right on the sparkling brooch that Aunt Elizabeth had pinned to her dress. It glittered so brightly that I saw its reflection in the studio windows.

Demoker saw it too. He stood stock still, staring at the bushes where we were hidden.

"Excuse me a moment," he said to the others, and disappeared through a door at the far end of the studio.

"He's seen us," I whispered.

At that moment another door opened and two enormous dogs came charging at us.

"Don't move," Aunt Elizabeth ordered.

Not that she needed to say that. I was almost paralyzed with fear as I stared at the two barking monsters before us, their teeth bared.

"May I ask what you are doing here?" said Demoker.

My aunt told him, "We've come for a Van Gogh and weren't allowed in. But since we've come such a long way we thought—"

"I couldn't care less what you thought," Demoker said threateningly. "I have no copies for you."

"But there must be at least fifteen hanging inside your studio," my aunt protested. "I'd like to buy one. Just tell me how much." She produced her money.

Demoker looked at it and laughed.

"My dear woman," he said, "my copies are no different from the real paintings."

"Which is why I've come to you," Aunt Elizabeth said, "and not to some bungler."

"They're no different from the real paintings in price either," Demoker went on.

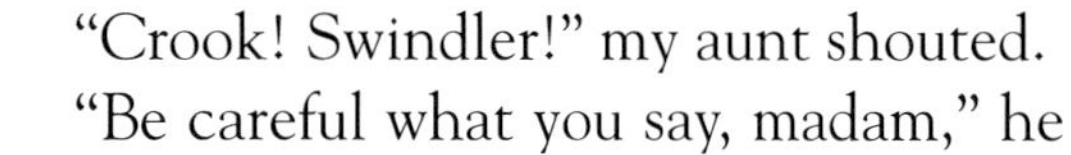

"Crook! Swindler!" my aunt shouted.

"Be careful what you say, madam," he said angrily. The dogs began to growl.

"I'm a professional, a genius. Those people inside know that. They're prepared to pay what I ask."

"Come along, Mark," my aunt said firmly. "There's nothing for us here."

"My sentiments exactly," Demoker said. He accompanied us down the drive and opened the gate we had climbed over.

It took us an hour and a half to walk back to the train station. Aunt Elizabeth didn't say a word all that time.

Nor did she talk about what had happened at Demoker's on the train. I could tell something was brewing, though. It was the way she was staring out the window. I knew she was disgusted at what we had seen and heard: vultures at a corpse, people to whom Van Gogh meant merely money and prestige. The starving, hardworking artist didn't exist for them. Only his world-famous paintings did. They didn't care about the man who had loved Japanese prints, the man who had worked himself into an early grave trying to capture ever more perfectly and strikingly the form and color of a garden, a church, a flight of stairs with flowers.

I sneaked a peek at Aunt Elizabeth. One look at her grim face made me know something big was about to happen.

When we got back to her house, she yanked the yellow flower paintings from the walls. Everything to do with Vincent she rolled up, tied into bundles, and crammed into two big trash bags.

Half an hour later we were on our way again. I puffed along beside her lugging the bags. We went to the pier. My aunt stared at the water for what seemed an eternity—not at the waves below us but at the horizon, where scraggly clouds met the sea. Where they touched, a yellow light gleamed. There was no sun, just that vivid light in the sky and the water like a moving reflection.

Suddenly, Aunt Elizabeth began to throw everything into the sea. The books fell into the water with a dismal splash. Aunt Elizabeth's unsuccessful paintings floated. They drifted farther and farther away until only the color could be seen—yellow dots on the gray sea.

We walked home in silence. Later, I saw that she had spared one picture—a portrait of a thin, red-bearded man. It stood in its frame on the cabinet among the family photographs.

Every now and then, Aunt Elizabeth looks at it and smiles the way you would at a photograph of a dear friend.

Vincent van Gogh

1853 Born March 30 in Zundert, Netherlands, the eldest son of the Protestant minister Theodorus van Gogh (1822–1885) and Anna Cornelia Carbentus (1819–1907).

1857 His brother Theo is born.

1866 After attending the village school and a boarding school in Zevenbergen, registers in September at the Rijks High School in Tilburg.

1868 Leaves the school in March, before the end of the second year for reasons unknown.

1869 In July Vincent works in The Hague as a junior assistant at Goupil & Company. Goupil sells original paintings by contemporaries and older artists and makes and sells reproductions.

1872 Starts a regular correspondence with his brother Theo.

1873 In July is transferred to Goupil in London. Falls in love for the first time, but his marriage proposal is rejected.

The house where Vincent was born.

Vincent at thirteen.

1874 In October is briefly sent to work at Goupil in Paris. Returns to London in December.

1875 In May is transferred to Paris.

1876 After being let go from Goupil in April, spends a short time as a teacher at a boarding school in England. Later teaches at another English school, where he is also the assistant chaplain. In December returns to the Netherlands and visits his parents in Etten.

1877 Works for the first few months at a bookstore in Dordrecht, Netherlands. Goes to Amsterdam to begin the two years of study needed to pass the national exam for entry into ministry training.

1878 In July quits his studies and returns to Etten. Moves to Brussels and completes a three-month training program to become an evangelist. In December begins his ministry in the Borinage, a mining region in southern Belgium.

1880 Stops working as an evangelist and moves back to Brussels. Decides to pursue art as a career. Meets the artist Anton van Rappard, with whom he becomes friends.

1881 In April returns to Etten. Falls in love with his niece Kee Vos-Stricker. He tries to win her heart, but his attempts come to nothing. In December he moves to The Hague.

1882 Meets Sien Hoornik, whom he uses as a model. Decides to marry her, but his family and friends disapprove. Attempts lithography for the first time in November.

1883 In September breaks off the relationship with Sien Hoornik and leaves The Hague. Goes to live with his parents in Nuenen in December.

1884 Rents an art studio in Nuenen, but lives with his parents. Meets Margot Begemann; nothing comes of their plans to marry.

1885 On March 26 Vincent's father dies unexpectedly. Not long after, produces the most famous painting from this period, *The Potato Eaters*. In November moves to Antwerp, Belgium, where he sees Japanese prints for the first time and begins his lifelong admiration of them.

1886 In January and February attends the art academy in Antwerp. In late February goes to Paris to live with Theo. For the next few months works in Fernand Cormon's studio. In summer Vincent and Theo move to the Rue Lepic. Comes into contact with Impressionist and Pointillist artists.

1888 In February leaves Paris for Arles. In September moves into the 'Yellow House.' From October to December, Paul Gauguin stays with him. Just before Christmas, cuts off part of his ear. Gauguin goes back to Paris.

1889 Vincent's wound heals, but he is still very disturbed. In April Theo marries Jo Bonger. A month later Vincent is admitted to the asylum in Saint-Rémy and stays there for the next year. His work is exhibited at the Salon of the Independents in Paris.

1890 In January the first issue of the *Mercure de France* includes an article by the critic Albert Aurier praising Vincent's work. In the same month Theo and Jo's only child is born and named Vincent Willem. Vincent leaves Saint-Rémy in May. After a short stay with his brother, he moves to Auvers, France. Meets Dr. Paul-Ferdinand Gachet. In early July visits Paris for the last time.

On July 27 Vincent shoots himself. Two days later he dies. He is thirty-seven years old. Theo van Gogh dies six months later.

ACKNOWLEDGMENTS

Vincent van Gogh Stichting/
Rijksmuseum Vincent van Gogh, Amsterdam
Harvest at La Crau, cover
The Weaver, 4
The Potato Eaters, 5
Crows in the Wheatfields, 7
Japonaiserie: The Flowering Plum Tree
(after Hiroshige), 11
Woman Sitting in the Café du Tambourin, 19
Pear Tree in Blossom, 24
View of Arles with Irises in the foreground, 25
Vincent's house in Arles, 26
Boats on the beach at Saintes-Maries, 28
Collection Rijksmuseum Kröller-Müller,
Otterlo, Netherlands
Self-portrait, 2
The Sower, 6
The Langlois Bridge with Women Washing, 8
Still life: Vase with Daisies and Dahlias, 22
Café terrace on the Place du Forum
in Arles, at night, 29
Still life: Sunflowers, 32
The Garden of Saint Paul's Hospital, 35
Road with Cypress and Star, 37
Collection Haags Gemeentemuseum,
The Hague
Self-portrait, Paris, 1880, 20
Still life of Pottery, Beer Glass, and Bottle, 20
Groninger Museum, Groningen, Netherlands
The Vicarage Garden at Nuenen, 41
Musée d'Orsay, Paris
La Ginguette, 14
Self-portrait, 21
Van Gogh's Bedroom in Arles, 27
The Church at Auvers, 36
Musée Rodin, Paris
Portrait of Père Tanguy, 17
Metropolitan Museum of Art, New York,
Sam A. Lewisohn Bequest
Madame Ginoux with books, 36
Museum of Modern Art, New York,
Abby Aldrich Rockefeller Bequest
Hospital Corridor at Saint-Rémy, 40
Courtauld Institute Galleries
(Courtauld Collection), London
Self-portrait with Bandaged Ear, 30
Christie's, London
Still life: Sunflowers, 13
Kunstmuseum, Winterthur, Switzerland
Roulin the Postman, 26
Museum für Ostasiatische Kunst, Cologne, Germany
Flowering Plum Tree near Kameido
(by Andô Hiroshige), 11

Letters:
The endpapers are fragments of letters from
Vincent to Theo with sketches of
The Potato Eaters and *Boats on the Beach*
Portfolio with letters from Vincent to Theo, 23
Envelope with letter from Vincent to Theo, 47

Photographs:
Tom Haartsen, Ouderkerk a/d
Amstel, Netherlands, 2, 6, 8, 29, 32
© ABC-press, Amsterdam, 12
© RMN, Paris, 14, 21, 27, 36 (left)
T. Strengers, 20 (right)
Municipal Archive, Nuenen/Harry Bakkers,
Eindhoven, Netherlands, 38
Office de Tourisme, Auvers-sur-Oise/Pierre Leprohon,
Cannes, France, 41 (top)
Vincent van Gogh Foundation/
National Museum Vincent van Gogh, 46 (right)
Municipal Archive, Zundert, Netherlands, 46 (left)
© Tjalke Bergsma, Netherlands, 47 (bottom)

First published as *Op zoek naar Vincent*
by Uitgeverij Ploegsma bv, Amsterdam, in 1990.

ISBN: 1-56288-300-3
Library of Congress Catalog Card Number: 92-72354

Printed in Mexico
by R.R. Donnelley & Sons Company.
0 9 8 7 6 5 4 3 2 1

Je ne m'en ferais pa

ce cas

Je travaille dans ce

rose violacé l'eau e